MELT FOR US

MOLLY DOYLE

CONTENT WARNING

This is a Dark Romance/Suspense, Reverse Harem Novella with MMF and MM scenes. MELT For Us contains mature and graphic content that may not be suitable for all audiences.

For a complete Content Warning list please visit my website.

TIMELINE

Book 1) Scream For Us (Novella) — Takes place on Halloween night.

Book 2) Full-length Novel (release: Early 2022) — Timeframe is from the morning after Halloween up until Christmas Eve. This is the full-length novel in the series, where all of your questions will be answered. This book is currently in the works!

Book 3) Melt For Us (Novella) — Fast forwards to Christmas & NYE!

Just to clarify, since the full-length novel is still in the works, you'll still be able to enjoy Melt For Us. This is another holiday-themed novella for you to read in the meantime! My Christmas gift to you all 🤍

CONTENTS

"Merry Christmas, you filthy animal.
And a happy New Year."

— *HOME ALONE 2*

PROLOGUE

"Quinn—" Jenna briefly pauses, gazing down at Ghost, Jason, and Michael from the second-story window. "Do you have any idea who they are?"

My breathing hitches, and my knees grow weak.

She turns back to me, eyes wide. "You need to be careful," she warns. "They're dangerous."

"Who are they?"

"The one you call Ghost," she begins, dropping the curtains. "That's Damien Sylvester."

Damien.

"Jason," she murmurs, releasing a small breath. "That's Jensen Peterson."

Jensen.

"And Michael," I urge, as a sudden chill sweeps through me.

Finally, her eyes meet mine. "Micah Henderson."

Micah…

CHAPTER 1

here are tall, wooden pillars and dark, polished hardwood floors beneath our feet. My gaze roams over the multicolored lights draped around the beautifully sculptured beams of the ceiling. It's evident from the Christmas décor that one of them had been here earlier to set this up. A smile claims my face at the thought of them planning this out just for me.

"No way," I rush out. "Whose place is this?"

"Ours," Damien says, resting his hand against the small of my back. "It's ours."

"And who set all of this up?" I ask, beaming with joy.

My gaze sets on Jensen.

"Don't look at me," he dismisses, holding up his hands.

Damien helps me out of my winter coat. "As much as I'd love to take credit for such a romantic gesture, it wasn't me," he admits.

"Micah," I exclaim, darting toward him as he drops his duffle bag to the ground. "I should've known it was you."

He lifts me from the floor, locks my thighs around his hips, and holds the back of my neck. "You said you love Christmas, so, I figured I'd do something special for you."

"You're amazing," I whisper, pressing my lips to his, breathing him in. "You're such a sweetheart." I kiss him forcefully, linking my arms around his neck, and parting my lips. His tongue brushes lightly against mine, and I melt inside. My heart feels so full. "Micah," I murmur, smiling with gratitude. "Thank you."

"No need for that," he dismissively says.

"This was a three-hour drive," I press. "Six hours of driving, and even more hours on top of that to set all of this up. Now it makes sense why you were gone all day yesterday. You did this just for me."

"How could you ever repay him?" Damien asks, sarcasm thick in his tone.

"Oh, I have some ideas," I reply, grinding my lower half against his waist.

A hushed moan escapes him.

"There's not much daylight left," Jensen lets out. "And something's missing."

"Oh?" I question.

"Liquor?" Micah asks, placing me back onto my feet before smacking my ass.

"You know I keep this place heavily stocked," Damien retorts, heading into the kitchen and opening the top cabinet. He retrieves a bottle of whiskey and four shot glasses, setting them onto the counter of the island. "Take a look around, Quinn. Make yourself at home."

Sunlight pours into the room through the wall entirely made of glass. The sun's rays warm my rosy cheeks, while I take in the sight of the woods and mountains out in the distance. Snow dances along the gusts of the wind, and it's a winter wonderland outside.

There's such a rustic feel to this cabin, and just knowing we are out in the middle of nowhere, together, a calm feeling washes over me. This is undoubtedly my happy place. I don't know how it could get any better than this.

"When's the last time we used them?" I overhear Jensen asking.

"It's been a while," Damien dryly responds. "Two years, maybe."

"There's a few canisters of gas in the shed. Grabbed some yesterday," Micah announces.

Making myself comfortable on the stool at the kitchen island, I lean my arms on the counter. "Gas for what?"

"Snowmobiles," Damien says, filling the glasses with bourbon up to the rim.

"No way!"

He cocks his head to the side, studying my reaction. "Excited?"

"Yes!"

Jensen hands me a shot. "To finding the perfect tree for Quinn," he toasts.

They all hold up their glasses to me, and we *clink*. Tossing back the whiskey, my throat immediately burns, and a strong blush settles on my face.

And I smile with gratitude as Damien pours us another round.

SOARING ON THE SNOWMOBILE, I tightly squeeze my arms around Micah's waist. We somehow gain even more momentum. Damien races past us, heading straight for a hill. An unexpected rush of adrenaline consumes me as I watch him take flight, hurdling through the cold, winter air.

He lifts himself into a standing position, turning back to look our way, waving for us to follow behind him. We make our way toward the edge of the woods. Slowing our speed, my gaze scans the beautiful Christmas trees of all different sizes.

Jensen follows closely behind, towing a sled that carries a chainsaw. In my family, we've always had a real tree for Christmas; however, this is the first time I've ever had the chance to choose one from the wild.

Damien slows, riding parallel to us. "Just say when," he instructs.

Smiling with excitement behind my helmet and face shield, I nod.

Suddenly, it begins to snow, and a shiver travels down my spine. Embracing the wintry wind, I hug Micah tight, waiting to catch the first glimpse of the perfect tree. Gliding over the fresh blanket of snow over the icy ground, the space around us falls silent.

We come to a stop, and I watch as Damien removes his helmet, retrieving a flask of whiskey from the inside of his coat.

"What about this one?" Jensen asks, pointing toward the tallest tree in sight.

"That's impossible," I say, holding back a laugh.

"Nothing's impossible," he says.

"We could make it work," Damien speaks up, tossing back the liquor before tossing the flask to Jensen.

"I found it!" I exclaim, removing my helmet and climbing off the seat. Shuffling my boots through the snow, I head toward the perfect tree. "This is it. *This* is the one."

Jensen lets out a dry laugh. "Well, this is unexpected."

"What do you mean?" I ask, turning to face them. They burst into laughter. "What's so funny?"

Damien dismounts his snowmobile, shaking his head.

"It's perfect," I argue.

"Look at the fucking branches," Jensen retorts.

"So, what?" I defensively ask. "It's perfect just the way it is. Don't make fun of it."

Micah laughs.

Hard.

"Not you, too, Micah," I snarl, joining in on the laughter with them. "Whatever. You said I get to choose which one I want, and I want this one."

"The princess shall have what the princess wants," Damien says, grabbing the chainsaw from the sled. "Don't be a brat."

"Shut up," I say under my breath.

Without warning, Damien grabs my jaw, tracing his gloved thumb over my lips. "What was that?" he asks, staring at me with piercing blue eyes, leaving my knees weak.

"You're the best," I playfully murmur, lustfully gazing up at him. "*Daddy*."

"Yeah." He crookedly grins, leaning into me. "That's what I thought."

They strap the tree to the sled the best they can, even though it's a lot bigger than we had initially anticipated. Soaring through the icy air, the wind blows. It's almost impossible to see more than just several feet ahead of us due to the thick blanket of snowflakes.

The daylight fades and the sun begins to set, which creates the most stunning scenery on the horizon.

"This is the most beautiful thing I've ever seen," I say.

Micah turns back to look at me. "I don't know about that," he replies.

"Okay. Name one thing more beautiful than this."

His hand grips my thigh, just above my knee. "You, Quinn," he tells me. "You."

My stomach flutters as I hold him tighter, dissolving against him.

CHAPTER 2

*B*y the time we reach the cabin, the blizzard has arrived with a vengeance. Damien and Jensen carry the tree into the house, while Micah and I park the snowmobiles in the dimly lit shed. Placing my helmet onto the nearest workbench, I watch in silence as he removes his. The black ski mask he's wearing catches me off guard and has me remembering how we met on Halloween night. Suddenly, I find myself tightly clenching my thighs.

His eyes lock with mine. Without warning, his hand catches my wrist. In one, swift motion, he pulls me against his chest. Grazing his hands along my back, they trail down to my ass, and he yanks me closer. Thrusting his hips forward, he slams my back against the cold, hard wall of the shed. Slipping his hands beneath my jacket and shirt, his cold hands cup my breasts, pinching my puckered nipples between his fingers.

"Micah," I softly moan, grabbing his straining erection, and rubbing him over his gray sweatpants.

"Fuck," he grunts, thrusting against my touch.

"Micah," I breathlessly whisper, as he rests his masked face in the crook of my neck, breathing me in.

"Fuck, baby," he sharply exhales, massaging my clit through my jeans with one hand, and tracing his thumb over my hardened nipples with the other.

He takes my hand, linking his fingers through mine, and drags me behind him as we exit the shed. Rushing through the snowy night, we scurry up the stairs leading to the back entrance of the cabin.

Micah shuts the door behind us with a loud slam, paying Damien and Jensen no mind as he lifts me into his arms. Placing my ass onto the dining room table, he pushes me onto my back. Pulling off my jeans and panties, he spreads my legs.

I'm a wet, quivering mess, begging to be fucked into oblivion.

From the corner of my eye, I see Damien and Jensen lifting the tree into the stand, when Micah grabs my ankles and yanks me to the edge of the table. His long, thick cock springs free as he lowers his sweatpants, resting them just below his ass.

He works his cock with one hand, and my clit with the other. Squirming against him, I whimper, shutting my eyes while my juices drip from my cunt.

"Fuck me, Micah," I desperately beg. "Please, fuck me."

With one, hard stroke he enters me, the table shaking back and forth with each savage thrust. He grips my hips, slamming into me relentlessly. Again. Again. And again. Breathing hard. Groaning. Biting out curses. Burying his fingertips into my thighs, bruising my skin.

"Yes," I cry out, writhing on the cold, hard surface of the table.

He strokes my inner walls, hitting just the right spot.

"Yes," I encourage. "Right there."

"Fuck," he groans, sinking into me over and over.

"Don't stop," I urge, my mouth popping open. "Yes. God, yes!"

"That's it, baby," he praises. "Fucking take it. Take this cock like a good girl."

My legs begin to quiver. "Harder," I beg.

His pace slows, and he slams into me hard. Thrust after thrust, he uses force.

"Like this, baby?"

"Yes," I whimper.

"Do you deserve to come?"

"Please. Yes. Please, Micah."

My orgasm rapidly builds. The moment he presses his thumb over my clit, I nearly come undone. Rubbing my clit in slow, torturous circles, he instantly throws me over the edge. My climax rips through my body, consuming me, while I ride out wave after wave of everlasting euphoria.

Curling my hands into fists at my sides, Micah continues his beautiful, yet merciless attack on my body. My inner walls spasm around his cock, as he stretches me wide, slamming into me with an urgency. Again, and again, jolting me back with each stroke.

"Fuck," he snarls behind his mask, eyes narrowed. "Good." *Thrust.* "Fucking." *Thrust.* "Girl."

My eyes roll into the back of my head.

"Yes, yes," I pant, while he firmly grips my waist, granting himself every ounce of control.

"Again," he orders, plunging deeper. "Now, Quinn. I'm not going to last much longer." He groans, lifting my leg between thrusts, and resting my ankle over his shoulder. "Come for me again, baby."

Another wave of my orgasm claims me, right on cue. It's almost too much for me to handle. The pleasure so intense, it's actually painful.

"That's it," he encourages, breathing hard. "Milk me dry, Quinn. Oh, *fuck*."

Throwing back his head, he finds his release with one final thrust.

"WHAT'S THE MATTER?" Damien asks me.

Staring at the bare branches of our Christmas tree, I sigh. "Nothing," I reply, forcing a grin.

Jensen wraps his arm around me, pulling me closer to him on the couch. "Don't lie."

"I guess I'm used to it being lit up."

Micah enters the room, carrying a box. "You really thought we forgot."

"Lights!" Kneeling beside Micah, I impatiently wait for him to cut it open. "Do you guys have any ornaments?"

He shrugs.

"Basement," Damien answers.

"We have any more wood?" Jensen asks, poking at the flames in the fireplace with the iron pointer. "Wood that isn't *wet*?"

"Quinn," Damien sarcastically accuses.

"You're hilarious," I say, rolling my eyes.

After plugging the first set of multicolored lights into an extension cord, Jensen hands me the strand. "Need any help?" he asks.

"Not yet," I tell him, placing the strand on the branches, starting at the bottom. "But I'll need your height once I get near the top."

Once we've finished decorating the tree with lights and ornaments, I snuggle up between Damien and Jensen on the couch, taking in the winding pathway of light from the base to the very top. The glow illuminates the deep green pine needles, and I breathe in the fresh aroma of sap and bark.

"It's perfect," I whisper, resting my head on Damien's shoulder.

He lightly brushes his fingers through my hair. "You did good."

"This is our first Christmas Eve together," I point out, my eyes searching his.

"And many more to come," he says, his voice promising.

"Can I be honest?"

Jensen's grip on my thigh tightens, as he gently strokes my skin in circular motions with his thumb. "We always expect honesty from you."

"I never expected this," I sheepishly admit.

Micah steps away from the fireplace, as the flames crackle and wood pops, concern for me displayed in his eyes.

"Before I was yours—"

"You were *always* ours," Damien sharply breathes, tightening his hold on me. "Let's make that very clear."

"Damien," Jensen warns.

His jaw twitches, and something darkens in his eyes. "I'm only stating facts."

"Us," I rush out, briefly hesitating. "I never expected us to end up together."

"You were bound to be with us, Quinn," Jensen says, intertwining his fingers through mine, kissing the back of my hand.

"We've lived in darkness for so long," Damien says, grazing his lips against the crook of my neck, trailing down to my collarbone. "You are the only light we have."

Micah moves behind the couch, massaging my shoulders and easing my tense muscles.

Placing my hand over his, I tilt my head back, meeting his gaze. He leans down, his lips mere inches from mine. He looks over every inch of my face, studying me. It's as if he's memorizing my every feature. He's never been so unreadable, so deep in thought.

"What?" I ask, barely any sound to my voice. "What is it?"

"Just admiring you." Micah changes his demeanor, stepping back before turning to Damien. "Ready?"

Damien nods once, standing.

And they disappear down the hallway.

"What was that about?" I wonder, looking to Jensen for answers.

He casually shrugs, pushing himself up from the couch and holding out his hand. "I have something to show you," he says, as I place my hand in his. "My favorite part of the cabin."

CHAPTER 3

*J*ensen leads me through a doorway toward the side of the house where we descend a small set of stairs, leading to what appears to be a sunroom. My eyes widen in disbelief as I take in the elegant sight. There are glimmering, white Christmas lights draped through the beams of the ceiling, lighting up the entire space above us, resembling a starry night.

From the warm ambiance of my surroundings, I'm left completely in awe.

"Are you serious," I whisper, more to myself than to him.

Jensen's hand rests on the small of my back. "Micah went all out decorating this place for you."

"I can't believe this!"

He laughs at my enthusiasm.

Two steps lead up to a wooden deck, supporting a large hot tub. A blue light illuminates the water. Steam rises as I ascend the steps, and humidity fills the space around us. It's a winter wonderland outside, snowflakes falling steadily from the night sky.

"This cabin is amazing."

He brings me against his chest. "I'm glad you like it," he breathes, tucking a loose strand of hair behind my ear. "As long as you're happy, I'm happy."

"Damien said it's ours, but who does it really belong to?"

Clenching his jaw, he remains silent for a moment. "It belonged to his parents," he says.

"Past tense," I say, inhaling an anxious breath.

He nods.

"He's never told me about them."

"I don't blame him."

Frowning, I avert my gaze to the water. "What happened to them?" I question, trying my best to sound casual.

"Quinn—"

"Sorry," I blurt out. "You're right. I shouldn't pry."

"Don't ask him," he warns.

Locking my eyes with his, a sudden feeling of concern washes over me. "Don't?"

"Don't," he sternly repeats. "I'm sure he will tell you eventually. When he's ready."

"You've never told me anything about your parents, either."

His lips part, and he weakly grins. "I don't have parents."

My heart immediately sinks. "Jensen," I apologetically rush out. "I'm so sorry—"

He brings me into him once more, and my body dissolves against his. "It's fine," he reassures me. "I don't mind. You have the right to ask questions."

Wrapping my arms around his waist, I breathe in his heady cologne. "It's just that, you know everything about my family," I begin. "And I know nothing about yours."

"I don't have a family, Quinn," he lets out, and tears fill my eyes. The moment he notices, his hold on me tightens. "It's fine. Really. I'm just not sure it would be the best conversation for Christmas Eve. It's pretty depressing."

"I don't want to make you talk about it."

"You're not forcing me," he objects, cupping my face with his hand. "I've never been asked about them. Never had anyone to tell."

"You know you can talk to me, right?"

"You're so selfless," he seductively breathes. "So kind. Caring. And so, so beautiful. You know that?"

His strong hands grip my waist as my hands find their way to his chest. His rippled muscles tense beneath my touch, and his breathing becomes shallow. Grazing my fingertips over his broad shoulders, I pull him closer, lifting my chin to gaze into his piercing eyes.

Grabbing the back of my neck, he leans closer. "You're perfect," he whispers, tightening his hold on me as I melt into his arms. "So goddamn perfect."

Jensen grabs a fistful of my hair, tilting my head. This grants him more access to kiss down my neck, his warm lips lingering over my collarbone. A quiet moan escapes me and my nipples strain against my lacey bra. Clenching my legs together, I attempt to ease the ache settling between my thighs. Although, I'm desperate for his touch.

For release.

He peels off my sweater, then my shirt, before dropping to his knees before me. His fingers swiftly unfasten the button and zipper of my jeans, working them down the curve of my hips, my thighs. Once they pool at my ankles, he stares up at me with a raging desire.

Gripping his shoulder to keep myself balanced, I step out of them, watching his gaze as it travels over every inch of my body. He groans as he caresses my legs, kissing the sensitive skin of my hip, grazing my red laced panties down my thighs. The feeling of his warm breath sends a shiver through me, while I run my hand through his disheveled hair.

"Fuck," he sharply exhales, pressing his lips against my stomach, kissing me tenderly.

His soft lips slowly make their descent. Kiss after kiss, love bite after love bite. He moves lower, and *lower*, until he's right there.

"Yes," I purr, spreading my legs as he kisses my clit. "Oh, *god*."

"Further," he impatiently orders.

I obey, spreading them wider. Granting him every bit of access.

"Good girl."

He takes me into his mouth, ravishing me. Flicking his tongue against my clit in the perfect rhythm, he grabs my ass, bringing me closer. My fingers yank on his hair and my body begins to quiver. Dipping his finger inside of me, he strokes my walls. Adding in another, he curls his fingers, finding just the right spot.

Crying out to him, he takes me between his teeth, lightly biting down. He sucks, licks, and flattens his tongue over my clit, increasing the speed as he fucks me with his thick, long fingers.

My breathing becomes labored while I grind myself against him, riding his face as he unhooks my bra, exposing my breasts. Reaching around to my chest, he twirls my puckered nipples between his fingers, and my orgasm claims me.

He grabs onto my ass, keeping me upright, and my body convulses. Complete euphoria from my orgasm courses through me, and my cries of pleasure echo through the room. Jensen continues to devour me, lapping up my juices, until eventually the space around us falls silent.

Tis the season for giving, and especially *receiving*.

Without warning, he stands, towering over my small frame. Jensen sweeps me off my feet, holding me bridal style in his arms. He carries me through the cabin, and my arms find their way around his neck. Anticipation from the unknown overtakes me.

Pushing open a door with his shoulder, we enter a master bedroom dimly lit by candles. The flickering flames appear to be coming from every direction, yet it's dark enough for me not to be able to make out anyone else in the room.

Jensen lowers me onto the bed, pressing my back into the mattress. "Don't move," he murmurs, warning me to obey.

And I nod.

With that, he turns away, dismissing himself from the room.

Suddenly, I'm on edge. Here I am, entirely naked, without anyone else in sight. My mind begins to wander as I allow my imagination to take over. It's evident they have something planned out, their own private agenda, and I don't have the slightest idea as to what that may be.

The silence is deafening.

My heart is drumming wildly.

Until unexpectedly, the door opens once more. Damien, Jensen, and Micah all stand before me wearing Santa hats.

Santa hats, *only*.

My nipples pucker at the festive sight.

Holy, not so silent, night.

"Close your mouth, Quinn," Damien taunts, his heavily tattooed, masculine body flexing as he approaches the bed.

"Tempting us," Jensen adds in, his cock twitching while he inches closer.

Micah plugs in a strand of Christmas lights into the wall beside the nightstand, a mischievous grin playing at the corner of his lips. He wraps the beginning of the strand around the left post of the headboard, while Jensen holds up my arm.

Another fantasy of mine is being brought to life.

"We made a list, little Quinn," Damien whispers beside my ear.

"We checked it twice," Jensen adds, twirling the strand of lights around my arm, pulling tight.

"And it turns out that—" Micah hesitates, binding my other arm as well. "Our pretty little slut has been naughty."

My face flushes as I pull hard on the strand, cutting off the circulation at my wrists. "What happens to naughty girls?"

Damien joins me on the bed, his hard, thick cock straining between my slick thighs. "Naughty girls get choked."

"Do it," I gasp, and a heated desire ignites within his eyes. "Choke me, daddy."

"I don't know if you're ready for this, princess," he warns, tracing his thumb over my lips.

Swallowing hard, I stare deeply into his eyes. "Ready for what?"

His face hardens. "The darkest part of me."

Blinking up at him, I fight away my fears. "Do it," I whisper. "I want all of you, Ghost, even your demons."

"Do you trust me, wholeheartedly?"

"Yes," I answer. "With everything in me."

"That's it, baby," he lets out, locking his fingers around my throat. "Don't fight it."

He applies more pressure, making it impossible for me to breathe. But I asked for this. I practically begged for this.

This is a feeling I'm not used to.

"Is that fear in those pretty green eyes?" he smugly asks, cocking his head to the side, studying me. His lips part as he takes in the vulnerable sight of me beneath his body, bound to the headboard and entirely helpless.

Breathless.

In response, I pull hard on the string of lights wrapped around my wrists. And to my own surprise, instead of panicking, I find myself smiling.

Egging him on.

"Yes," he praises, tightening his grasp, as I begin to slip further and further away. Suddenly, he eases the pressure. "Fuck." He moans under his breath. "You look so fucking hot with my hand around your throat, Quinn. I can't take it."

"More," I eagerly plead, writhing against him.

"Naughty girl, you thought that was it?" he asks, taunting me, as he cuts off my air supply once more.

Harder. Relentless. Showing me not even the slightest bit of mercy. Oxygen demands to fill my deprived lungs. Even swallowing is impossible. My heart rate accelerates, pounding hard in my chest, while his eyes flicker with amusement.

Watching me closely, I begin to struggle beneath him, and my vision becomes blurry. Damien slowly sinks into me, easing the pressure on my throat, finally granting me permission to breathe.

"Fuck," he sharply groans, shooting me an intense stare, thrusting deeper. "You good, baby?"

"Yes," I gasp for air, consumed with a high I wasn't expecting. "Again," I urge.

Jensen and Micah step closer, watching us intently.

"Oh, I'm not finished with you yet, Quinn," Damien breathes, tossing the Santa hat onto the floor and pulling on his Ghostface mask instead. "We're just getting started."

Locking his tattooed hand around my throat once more, he presses down, choking me harder. My head becomes light. My eyes begin to water. Adrenaline courses through me as Jensen and Micah pull on their masks as well, bringing me back to Halloween night.

"Keep your eyes open for me," he instructs. "Do not break eye contact unless you've had enough. If it's too much for you."

But it's not.

It's far from that.

A feeling of utter euphoria washes over me. Damien sees it when he looks into my eyes. I'm starving for more. He slams into me forcefully, crushing his weight against my body. Curling his fingers tighter around my neck, his hips slam against my pelvis repeatedly.

He fucks me without emotion. Savagely. Bruising my skin from the sheer force behind each thrust. And he gets off on it, groaning loudly, as I watch his chest rise and fall with each uneven breath.

My eyelids become heavy, and he notices, releasing the pressure at once.

"Ghost," I breathlessly plead, desperate for more. "I'm so close." I moan, tugging on the lights as they cut at my wrists. "*Please*."

He smiles deviously, thrusting into me harder, jolting me back from the force.

"You look so pretty with your face streaked in tears," he sadistically says, wrapping another strand of multicolored lights around my neck.

Choking me with them.

Micah steps closer. "Damien—"

"She asked for this," he cuts him off, pressing down on my throat, slowly increasing the pressure. "She's so—" *Thrust.* "Fucking—" *Thrust.* "Wet."

Staring into the dark eyes of his mask, my orgasm rips through me, consuming every ounce of my being. And he *knows*.

"That's right," he bites out. "Fucking come for me."

My endorphins are released as my body kicks into fight or flight. I have never experienced this level of intensity before, and as soon as I look away from the eyes of his mask, he releases my throat.

"Good girl," he praises, sinking into me again and again, my inner walls sucking hard at his cock. "*Fuck.*" Finding his release with one final thrust, he collapses onto me, his strong body thick in sweat. "You took that so well, little Quinn." He lightly strokes my hair, soothing me as I catch my breath, before pushing himself up from the bed. "I'm so fucking proud of you."

Micah unwraps the lights from around my neck, and my arms, caressing my wrists to ease the discomfort. Seeing him back in his mask from Halloween night sends a chill down my spine. Flashbacks begin to take over, until suddenly, he joins me on the bed.

Resting on his back, he pulls me onto him, his straining erection pressed against his defined abs. Straddling his waist, I position the rosy head of his cock at my entrance, slowly sinking onto him inch by inch.

"Fuck," Micah grunts, lifting his hips from the mattress, burying himself deeper.

Jensen climbs behind me, wrapping the strand around my arms pinned at my sides, lighting me up in red. "Can you break free?" he asks beside my ear.

"No," I say.

"Good."

He bends me forward as I arch my back. Micah wraps his arms around me, holding me tight. Grinding my clit against his pelvis sends a spark of pleasure through me, while Jensen lubes my ass, preparing me for his invasion. Stretching me wide with his fingers, I move faster, even though my arms being bound leaves me immobile.

"Yeah," Jensen encourages. "Fuck my fingers with your tight little ass."

Micah wraps his arms around my back and drills into me from the mattress, while Jensen presses the tip of his cock against my back entrance. Thrusting forward, he slowly fills me.

"Yes," I cry out, entirely consumed by them.

Jensen tightens his grip on my hips as he pounds into me from behind, while Micah continues to take control beneath me, both in the perfect rhythm.

A muffled whimper escapes my lips.

"Fuck," Micah sharply exhales. "I'm not going to last much longer hearing those sexy little cries."

"More," I beg, stretched wide.

"You want all of us?" Damien questions, slowly stroking his cock. "I could fuck you all night. Again. Again, and *again*."

Squirming against Jensen and Micah's warm bodies, I moan, "I want all of you."

"Beg," Micah commands, buried to the hilt.

"Please," I helplessly whine, rolling my hips. "Please, I'm begging. More. All of you."

Micah's fingertips dig into my thighs. "She wants more," he breathes, plunging himself deeper with each stroke. "Let's give it to her."

Damien stares down at me with hunger. "So goddamn needy." He pries open my mouth with his thumb, before guiding his cock past my lips. "Suck," he commands, shoving himself into the back of my throat, as I gag. "Yes. Choke on daddy's dick. *Fuck*."

Gathering the loose strands of my hair, he brushes them away from my face.

"You're so good at sucking my cock."

As he pumps further into my mouth, all I can think of is air. I need *air*.

I'd give anything in the world to watch this as a bystander. Here I am, bound with Christmas lights, getting railed and gagged by my three masked men.

And even better, we all come together.

It couldn't get any more festive than this.

CHAPTER 4

S everal hours later, the blizzard intensifies, as we all snuggle together on the couch in the spacious living room. The flames dance erratically with the gusting wind from the chimney, whistling and crackling.

Resting my head on Jensen's lap, I take in the beauty of our Christmas tree, twinkling and lighting up the dark room. Memories of my last Christmas Eve flood through my mind, and the more I fight them away, the stronger they seem to flash back.

Damien caresses my leg, bringing me back to reality. "Are you okay?" he asks.

I remain silent.

Micah scoots closer, now shoulder to shoulder with Jensen, as he gently strokes my hair. "What's the matter?"

Jensen grips my jaw, turning my head and forcing me to look at him. "You're never this quiet," he points out, humorously.

A small laugh escapes me.

His eyes narrow. "Usually, we can't get you to shut the fuck up."

Rolling my eyes, I pull away, turning onto my side. "I'm fine," I lie.

"You can't lie to us, Quinn," Damien retorts. "We see right through you."

"It was a memory," I reply, shaking it off. "Just a stupid memory."

"Care to elaborate?" Jensen asks.

"She doesn't want to share," Micah interrupts, catching me off guard. "Let it be."

"Yeah? She can speak for herself."

"Get fucked."

"Enough," Damien orders, edginess in his tone.

Without thinking it through, I inhale a deep breath, squeezing my eyes shut. "Last Christmas, I was talking to this guy."

An eerie silence fills the space around us, until there's a dull ringing that settles in my ears.

"Oh?" Jensen urges.

"We went on a few dates," I begin, barely any sound to my voice. "He seemed like a really nice guy. Took me to fancy restaurants. Bought me random gifts here and there." Briefly hesitating, I hug the blanket tighter to my chest. "Until he started calling and texting me all the time. Asking where I was and who I was with."

Damien leans forward, tensing his body as he firmly grips my legs.

Micah continues to stroke my hair.

Jensen's breathing becomes labored.

"And not believing me when I told him," I quietly add in, letting out a nervous laugh. "I'm so fucking stupid."

"Don't say that," Damien spits out. "Don't you ever call yourself stupid."

"I ignored all of the red flags. Every. Single. One," I speak slowly, looking away. "I never should have gone to that Christmas Eve party with him."

Damien moves my legs from his lap, and rushes to his feet. "No," he exhales, pacing the room. "Don't fucking say it, Quinn. Don't you fucking tell me—"

"Damien," Micah stammers, joining him beside the tree, grabbing onto his shoulder.

Damien swats him away. "He's dead," he coldly states. "He's fucking dead."

"Quinn," Jensen whispers, locking his eyes with mine. "What happened?"

Tears fill my eyes.

"Quinn," he urges, taking my face between his hands. "What did he do to you?"

As I quickly sit upright, Micah kneels before me, resting his hands on my legs just above my knees. "It's alright," he softly tells me. "If you don't want to talk about it, we understand. But, if you do, just know that we're here for you."

Wetness coats my cheeks as I take his hands in mine. "I said no," I let out, my voice cracking. "I told him to stop. That I didn't want to."

Damien turns his back to me, masking his reaction.

"He hurt you," Jensen murmurs.

"We were both really drunk," I dismissively say, pushing myself up from the couch. "It was nothing. And it's in the past now, anyways. I'm over it."

Turning on my heel, I exit the room, making my way toward the kitchen. The sound of their footsteps behind me sends a rush of adrenaline through me. I'd do anything to take back that night. I'd do anything to be able to go back in time and change it.

To fight him off harder.

Anything.

"It's okay, Quinn," Micah says from over my shoulder. "You're okay now."

"You're safe with us," Jensen adds in.

"Don't fucking give her that shit," Damien bites out. "She needs to get angry."

"The fuck is wrong with you, man?" Micah demands. "She's gone through enough."

Gripping the edge of the countertop, I tightly shut my eyes. Damien's right.

He couldn't be any *more* right.

"She needs to stop lying to herself," Damien presses. "Quinn, it wasn't *nothing*. That fucking low-life piece of shit forced himself onto you. You said no. You told him to stop. That bastard raped you."

"He raped me," I echo in a whisper.

"I'm sorry, baby," he painfully says. "I'm so fucking sorry. You need to let yourself feel it. I can see the hatred and anger burning in your eyes. You've held it in for too long, baby. You need to let it out."

"But, how?" I nearly beg.

He steps closer; his jaw clenched tight. "Let us help you," he cautiously says.

Micah steps between us, bringing me into his arms.

"No," I spit out.

Micah stumbles back, staring at me with confusion. "No?"

"I said, no," I repeat, loudly, fisting his shirt at his chest and pulling him closer.

Gazing down at me with confusion, his eyes immediately narrow. "Quinn—"

"Stop!"

Micah jumps back, leaning his back against the counter and staring at me with horror.

Damien steps closer. "Tell us what you want from us, Quinn," he softly says.

"I want to feel empowered," I explain, trying my best to make them understand. "Instead of feeling helpless and ashamed."

"What can we do for you?" he asks.

"I don't want to feel like a victim anymore."

"You want to act it out with us," Jensen lets out, attempting to wrap his head around it. "Except this time, you know that you have every ounce of control."

"Am I crazy?" I ask, my voice cracking.

"No," Damien rushes out. "This is really what you want?"

"Yes."

"We need a safe word," he firmly states. "What will it be?"

"Mistletoe."

"Are you sure about this?" he asks again.

"Yes," I answer.

"Do you have any limits?"

I shake my head. "No."

They take a moment, exchanging silent stares. Finally, they nod in acceptance.

"Okay, Quinn. This time, you're in control," Damien says, before his eyes darken. "*Run*."

CHAPTER 5

DAMIEN

*Q*uinn takes off, pushing off the doorway and disappearing down the dark hall. Clenching my jaw tight, anger cripples me. My teeth feel as if they're seconds away from shattering. There's only one thing I'm sure of at this moment.

I'll hunt this guy down.

I'll find him.

And I'll rip his fucking throat out with my teeth.

"What is this?" Micah harshly asks me. "Why do you want her to live through this again?"

"Her being taken advantage of once isn't good enough for you?" Jensen angrily demands. "She has to experience it twice?"

"You don't get it," I shoot back. "This is what *she* wants. You heard her."

Jensen steps back, uncertainty claiming his face. "I'm out."

Micah's eyes narrow. "She chose a safe word," he breathes, running his hand through his hair. "That was her way of giving consent."

"We need to find this guy," Jensen states.

"We will," I state.

"Do we even know his name?" Micah questions.

"Not yet. But we will."

Jensen strides toward the doorway.

"You're bailing?" I call out.

"Grabbing us masks," he responds. "You know I'd never bail on her."

Micah remains motionless in the kitchen, his gaze fixated on the hardwood floor beneath our feet.

"You good?" I ask, gripping his shoulder. "You don't have to do this."

He immediately looks up, setting his pained eyes on mine. "I'd do anything for her."

And I nod.

We wouldn't just give her the world. We'd give her the skin off our bones.

Anything for Quinn.

Pulling the black mask down over my face, I take the lead down the pitch-black hallway, the only source of light coming from the Christmas tree and fireplace. Catching a glimpse of a figure from the corner of my eye, I come to realize it's just my shadow reflecting on the wall.

"Come out, come out, little Quinn," I quietly taunt.

Micah strides out of the bedroom and shakes his head.

"You can't hide from us forever," Jensen sneers, disappearing through the doorway of the guest bedroom.

The wind howls through the chimney, sending the tall flames into a frenzy, and the strands of lights on the tree begin to flicker.

Micah nudges me with his elbow, gesturing with a slight nod over to the couch. We slowly creep our way toward her, the small shadow on the wall giving her away. Until, suddenly, there's a loud creak from the floor with my next step forward.

She rushes to her feet, pushing off the wall with force allowing her a head start. We chase after her through the dark house, and just as we turn a sharp corner, I catch her wrist.

Trying desperately to pull herself away, I gain full control, wrapping my arms around her petite frame. When suddenly, she backhands me right in the face, before making another run for it down another hall.

Jensen smirks once he takes notice of my bloody lip. "Feisty," he remarks.

Micah steps beside me. "You good?"

Wiping the blood from the corner of my mouth, I crookedly grin. "Never been better."

The basement door has been left agape. We slowly descend the stairs, the sound of our footsteps putting the silence to an end.

And there she is, her back and palms pressed firmly to the wall.

"Nowhere else to hide, little Quinn?" I taunt, forcing myself into character. For *her*.

Anything for her.

"Leave me alone," she stammers, releasing a shaky breath.

"You fucking hit me," I laugh, mocking her.

"Did I?"

"You can stop this," I assure her. "Just use your safe word and it's over."

"Don't fucking pity me," she snaps, glaring into my eyes as we approach her. "I can handle this, and you know it."

Stepping forward, I leave her cornered, trapping her to the wall with my arms on both sides of her head. "Well, then," I breathe, kicking open her legs. "You better put up one hell of a fight."

There's a spark within her beautiful green eyes. "What are you waiting for?"

Locking my fingers around her wrists, I lift her arms, pinning her to the wall. Leaning my body into her, she begins to struggle, almost breaking out of my grasp. Tossing her over my shoulder, she kicks her legs and flails her arms, before I place her onto the pool table.

Jensen and Micah hold her down by her arms while I settle my waist between her legs. She fights us hard, giving every ounce of strength she can muster.

Yet, she gets nowhere.

"Let me go," she shouts, writhing her arms, trying to break free.

"Not a chance," I say, removing her pajama bottoms and letting them fall to the floor. Arching an eyebrow, I let out a low rumble of a laugh. "No panties." Spreading her thighs with my hands, I drown in the sight of her pink, glistening pussy, wanting nothing more than to fucking devour her. "You want me to taste this sweet little cunt, don't you?"

"No," she moans, her breathing hitching.

Leaning down, I bury my face between her slick thighs, and a whimper of desperation escapes her. Pressing my tongue flat against her clit, I lick her teasingly, savoring my favorite meal. She bucks her hips, cries out, and then tries to pull away.

"Hold her fucking still," I demand, yanking her to the edge.

Jensen and Micah slam her arms against the pool table, adjusting their positions to grant them a better grip.

"Stop," she urges, as I slip my hands beneath her thigh, cupping her ass with my hand. "I don't want this!"

Dipping my tongue inside her tight hole, I breathe hungrily against her flesh, reaching inside my sweatpants to pull out my dick.

"No," she cries out, tensing against me. "Fucking stop! Stop! *Stop*!"

"Damien," Micah snaps, unsure.

Lifting my gaze from her pussy, I set my eyes on his, flicking my tongue over her clit. Making a show of it. Harder, faster, finding her favorite rhythm that she can never seem to get enough of.

"No," she pants, grinding herself against my mouth. "Don't let me come."

"Don't tell me what to fucking do," I groan, thrusting two fingers inside her with one hand and stroking my cock with the other. "You're going to fucking come for me."

Forcing her arms above her head, they pin her down with a bruising grip. Standing tall, I tower over her, thrusting my cock inside of her with one, long stroke. Not even giving her the time to adjust to my size, I fuck her without any shred of emotion.

I fuck her like I *hate* her.

But, oh God, how I...

Without warning, she screams. Loud. So loud, I'd be worried if we had any neighbors. But we don't. We're in the middle of nowhere, where nobody can hear her cries.

"Go on," I tease, forcefully slamming into her, again and again. "Nobody can hear you."

She lets out more screams, and her pussy clenches tight around my dick, letting me know she's right there. Reaching into my pocket, I pull out my knife. Pressing the tip of the blade against her throat, she becomes motionless, suddenly terrified to move.

To struggle.

"Now be a good little slut, and fucking come for me," I command, rocking my hips as I thrust into her mercilessly. "Before I carve each of our initials into your skin as an infinite reminder of who you belong to."

Suddenly, her eyes lock with mine. "Do it," she challenges.

"Fuck," Jensen says under his breath.

"Don't tempt me, Quinn," I sharply breathe, slowing my strokes.

"Fucking do it," she cries, real tears.

My tainted heart sinks. I'll fucking kill him. I'll kill him for hurting her.

"Please," she chokes out, writhing beneath me. "I'm begging you."

Grazing the tip of the blade at the curve of her hip, I narrow my eyes. "Here?"

She impatiently nods. "Do it!"

"This is crazy," Micah objects, pressing a lingering kiss on her lips. "You're fucking crazy, Quinn; you know that?"

"Please," she pleads, until Jensen leans down next, crushing his mouth on hers.

Silencing her.

Pressing the blade into her skin, she flinches from the pain, lifting her entire body off the pool table. They pin her down once more, holding her tight, ignoring her screams which soon turn into cries of absolute pleasure.

Carving out each line, blood trickles, yet I remain buried inside of her at the same time. Stretching her wide, consuming her. Cutting her. Claiming her.

Thrust. Cut. Thrust. Cut.

Again, and again.

DS

MH

JP

"Yes," she moans out, arching her back.

Her inner walls tighten around my pulsating cock as her orgasm swallows her whole. Her body spasms, her pretty mouth pops open, and she tilts her head back while her endorphins rage through her. The pain. The pleasure. The mixture of them together.

She loves it.

She can't get enough.

And I drop the knife, emptying myself inside her. Thrust after thrust, I send her body further up the table with each deliberate stroke. Jensen and Micah release her arms, yet she doesn't move an inch. Tears leak from the corners of her shut eyelids.

"Quinn," I breathe, kissing the scars on her wrist. "It's over, Quinn."

Sneaking my arm beneath her back, I sit her up, before bringing her against my chest. She holds onto me so tight, like I'm the only solid thing in her universe.

And she sobs.

All three of us embrace her, comforting her the best we can.

"Thank you," she whispers, wrapping her arms around Jensen and Micah, pulling them into our embrace. "Thank you."

"It's okay, baby," Micah assures her, lightly stroking her hair.

"We got you," Jensen promises.

"You're safe now," I nearly whisper, pressing my forehead to hers. "Nobody will ever hurt you again."

I'll make sure of it.

And if they so much as even try... they'll meet their end.

CHAPTER 6

Bright rays of light beam in through the arched floor-to-ceiling window. Curled up together in the softest of blankets, tattooed arms yank me closer. Rolling onto my side, I take in the sight of Micah sound asleep beside me.

Jensen turns onto his side, facing us, and drapes his arm over Micah's chest. Snuggling into his embrace, they comfort each other in their sleep. Resting my chin on Micah's broad shoulder, I press myself against him, entangling our legs as I savor the warmth of his body.

Within seconds, his eyes flutter open, and a slight grin plays at his lips. Lightly stroking my arm with his fingertips, goosebumps rise on my skin. Rocking my hips against him, I breathe in the lingering scent of his cologne.

With a slight turn of his head, he presses his lips on mine. My head becomes light as he kisses me tenderly, brushing his tongue over the seam of my lips. Jensen turns away from us in his deep slumber. Micah rolls onto me, cupping the side of my face with his hand.

Our tongues collide, and he fights for control. He gropes my breasts, grazing his thumb over my puckered nipple before slipping his hand between my legs. A hushed moan catches in my throat when he finds my clit, massaging me in slow, precise circles. Teasing my entrance with slippery fingers, he exhales a sharp breath, taking my bottom lip between his teeth.

"Fuck," he whispers, dipping his finger inside of me. "Such a wet girl."

"Yes," I purr, arching my back, and pressing my breasts against his chest.

Micah adds in another finger, and curls them, stroking my g-spot. Every nerve ending is on edge. He knows just where to touch me, ensuring I fall apart beneath him. My breathing hitches once his lips find my neck, lightly grazing over the sensitive flesh beneath my ear.

"You want to get fucked, pretty girl?" he breathes, his erection growing between my already drenched thighs. "Turn over," he commands. "Now."

Without even giving me a chance, he flips me onto my stomach, pulling me back until I'm on my knees. Rubbing the rosy head of his cock up and down my wet slit, I push back on him, aching for more.

Micah enters me with one, hard stroke. My body jolts forward from the force of each thrust, my pussy clenching him tightly. He smacks my ass, leaving red handprints on my flesh as he sinks inside of me deeper. Reaching between my legs, he presses down on my clit, and my legs begin to shake violently.

"That's it," he urges, pushing into me harder. "Come undone for me."

"Oh, God," I moan, as my orgasm entirely consumes me.

"Such a good girl."

"I see you started without me," Jensen unexpectedly murmurs, moving onto his knees behind Micah. "Lean forward."

My heart instantly hammers as a few drops of lube trickle onto my leg, and I realize it's not being used on me.

Micah leans forward, pressing the front of his body against my back. "Fucking hell," he groans, becoming still inside me. "Oh, *fuck*, Jensen."

"You like that?"

"Fuck yes."

Jensen forcefully rocks the bed. "Yeah?"

"You know I do," he grunts.

Jensen slams into his ass, over and over, taking him without mercy. Rumbling groans and the sound of skin smacking fills the room. Micah pushes back against Jensen's throbbing cock, meeting him with each stroke, and I reach between my legs to cup his balls.

"Yeah, baby," he whispers beside my ear, pushing me flat onto my stomach.

Damien enters the room and leans against the doorway, watching eagerly.

Micah kisses down my neck, shoulder, and back, while sinking into me repeatedly. Squeezing my eyes shut, I tightly grip the sheets, stifling my moans by biting the pillow.

Oh, God.

My breathing quickens while his lips brush my neck, his hand tugging hard on my hair. Micah takes my wrist, guiding my hand between my thighs.

"Touch yourself, baby," he mutters through sharp breaths. "Come for me. Again."

"Fuck," Jensen bites out, pumping into his ass harder. Faster. "You feel so fucking good."

Micah's body tenses, collapsing onto me as I climax again.

Groaning heavily, they find their release at the same time, coming *hard*. I've never been so turned on in my life.

"Merry." *Thrust*. "Fucking." *Thrust*. "Christmas."

THE DELICIOUS AROMA of sizzling bacon, corned beef hash, and maple syrup fills the air. Gazing out through the large window of the kitchen, I'm left with an overwhelming feeling of Christmas joy. Last night was a game changer for me. It's as if a huge weight has been lifted, and I can finally breathe again. The sky is bright, and a white blanket of snow covers the ground, flurries now coming down light.

I can't even remember the last time I've felt this happy. This content.

This adored.

"How'd you sleep, princess?" Damien asks, pouring me another cup of coffee.

Meeting his eyes, I grin. "That bed is way too comfortable," I reply, taking another piece of crispy bacon. "It's dangerous how comfortable it is."

"I'm fucking stuffed," Jensen mumbles, scooting his chair away from the table.

"We must've lost power overnight," Micah brings up, dropping his plate in the sink. "Woke up around six and it was so cold I could almost see my breath."

"Well, the heats back on," Damien says, sipping his coffee. "We should have more wood out in the sunroom."

Jensen dismisses himself, leaving his empty plate on the table.

"What am I, your fucking maid?" Micah complains, cleaning the dishes.

"I'm going to start the fire," he retorts, shooting him a quick glare. "I'll grab it after. Relax."

Laughing under my breath, I attempt to cool off my coffee by blowing on it.

"You think it's funny?" Micah asks.

And I nod, holding back more laughter.

"I'll remember this," he playfully says, shaking his head. "What are our plans for today?"

Damien shrugs. "Must've gotten at least two feet of snow. They haven't even started plowing the roads. We're stuck here for a while."

"That's fine with me," I happily say, staring out the window once more. "It's so beautiful."

"There's not much to do around here. Way too many tourists," Micah explains, until I interrupt him.

"This is the best location ever. In the White Mountains, right off the Kancamagus Highway."

Jensen returns, holding several logs of wood against his chest.

Damien smirks, staring at me with intense eyes. "Would you like to live here someday?"

"Yes!" I exclaim. "There's just something about this cabin. It feels like home."

"Well, then," Jensen laughs as he walks by, with no humor intended. "We're going to need a bigger bed."

"IT'S TIME, LITTLE QUINN," Damien says.

"Time for what?"

"Time to unwrap your presents," Micah replies, unfastening the button of his jeans.

"Do you want to know what I really want?" I ask them.

Jensen reaches behind his shoulder and pulls his shirt over his head, watching me intently.

"What do you want, little Quinn?" Damien asks from across the room.

"I want full control over all three of you," I announce. "You do exactly as I say."

Damien, Jensen, and Micah stand before me, observing my every move. Taking in my request. Silent as can be.

Until Micah steps forward, dropping to his knees.

"Do what you want with me," he breathes. "For you, I'll do anything."

Jensen joins in, kneeling beside him, vulnerably gazing up at me. "Anything," he agrees.

My eyes set on Damien. And without any hesitation, he kneels, before crawling over to me.

"Look at us, your little pets, sitting at your feet," he says. "Use me, Quinn. Use all of us. With you, we have no boundaries."

"Good boys," I praise, running my fingers through Micah's hair, still damp from our shower. "Now, stand."

He obeys.

As soon as Damien and Jensen begin to stand, I firmly grip their shoulders, pushing them back down. "No," I scold, clicking my tongue. "Just Micah."

He towers over my small frame, staring submissively into my eyes.

Skimming the hem of his jeans with my fingertips, I give them a small tug. "I want these off," I say, confidence bursting through me. "Now."

Within seconds, he pulls them down, stepping out from them before kicking them off to the side. The large bulge of his erection twitches with anticipation beneath his boxers.

Rubbing his cock over the thin material, I eagerly grin. "These, too."

He pulls them down, slowly, and his cock springs free. The room is so quiet; all you can hear is the crackling wood in the fireplace. Micah waits patiently for his next instruction. I never expected them to give me so much power. To submit to me.

It goes straight to my head as I take full control.

"On the couch," I order.

He obeys.

"Touch yourself."

Wrapping his tattooed fingers around his shaft, he slowly strokes himself from tip to base, cupping his balls with his other hand. A quiet moan catches in his throat as he watches me strip off my clothes.

"Good," I murmur, leaning onto the couch, and straddling his waist. "You're my toy. I'll do what I want with you. Do you understand?"

"Yes, baby," he impatiently whispers, firmly gripping my thighs.

Positioning the tip of his cock at my entrance, I slowly lower myself onto him, accepting him inch by inch.

Locking my fingers around his wrists, I lift his arms, pinning them to the couch. Rolling my hips, and grinding my clit against his pelvis, I ride him with an urgency.

As if my life depends on it.

Entirely lost in the moment, my mind wanders, and time passes by. Flashbacks of Micah and Jensen together earlier this morning replays in my head, again and again. My pussy clenches tighter around him. My inner thighs are completely drenched with my juices as I bounce onto him with force, my ass smacking against his bare thighs.

"Oh, fuck," he roars, his hands turning into tight fists.

"Damien," I call out, breathlessly, gesturing with a nod to the spot beside us. "Get over here."

He quickly makes his way to the couch, sitting beside us in silence, his mouth agape as he watches.

"I'm so wet," I whine, throwing back my head in ecstasy, and crying out to them.

"Oh, fuck," Jensen groans from behind me.

"Do you know why?" I question, coming down harder, digging my nails into his wrists.

"Why, baby?" he hisses, locking his eyes with mine.

"I can't stop thinking about earlier," I moan, the friction from my clit rubbing against his pelvis throwing me closer to the edge. "You and Jensen," I add in. "It was so fucking hot, Micah. Knowing he was fucking you like that."

"You liked that?" he purrs, bucking his hips from the couch, matching my movements.

"Oh, God, yes," I helplessly cry, coming hard, sitting back on him as he stretches me wide. "I loved it."

"Tell us what you want," he breathes, taking his bottom lip between his teeth. His biceps flex, and his body tenses. "Tell us."

"Again," I demand. "This time, I want to watch."

Climbing off his lap, Damien pulls me onto his waist, wasting no time in lowering me onto his long, thick cock next. From the way he was fucking himself with his hand as he watched the feral sight of me, I know he's ready to explode.

Micah rushes to his feet, shoving Jensen onto the couch. Kneeling beside us, he braces the edge of the backrest, as Micah spits on his cock, even though it's already coated with my cum. He thrusts forward, slow at first, before pounding into him savagely.

My heart is hammering as I watch. My body is drenched with sweat. My toes begin to curl, and my eyes roll into the back of my head, as wave after wave of another intense orgasm bursts through me.

Damien grips my hips, bruising my delicate flesh, and slams me down forcefully. Over, and over, and over again.

"You're such a dirty girl," he bites out, bringing me down faster. "You're going to make me come so fucking hard, baby."

"Come for me, daddy."

"Fuck."

Spilling himself inside of me in long spurts, he sneaks his arm around my back, nuzzling his face in the crook of my neck.

"*Ours*," he breathes against me.

CHAPTER 7

"*J* thought we said no gifts?" I question.

Jensen laughs, gesturing to a large box under the tree with candy cane wrapping paper. "No, *you* said that, not us."

"But I didn't get you guys anything—"

"You've already given us something," Micah objects.

Sheepishly grinning, I shake my head in disbelief. "What did I give you?"

"You," Damien states, as a blush settles on my cheeks. "You gave us *you*."

"And you're the best damn gift," Jensen says, handing me my first present as I make myself comfortable on the floor. "This one's from me."

Anticipation overwhelms me as I tear off the wrapping paper, losing my mind once I realize it's the designer bag I've been obsessing over for the last year. It's extremely expensive, and I could never afford it, especially after all the money I've spent on purchasing new books.

"No way," I shriek, examining the beauty of seeing it in person. "Are you serious? Jensen, are you serious?"

"Yup."

"You're amazing," I blurt out, rushing to my feet and leaping into his arms. "I'm so happy! It's so beautiful!"

He holds me close, smiling. "Glad you like it."

"Like it? I love it!" I exclaim, pressing my lips against his. "Thank you."

"Tough act to follow," Micah dryly mumbles, handing me a small-sized box.

A countless number of thoughts rush through my head as to what it could be. Unwrapping the paper and lifting the lid, I'm suddenly left speechless. Gazing down at the diamond necklace in awe, I marvel at its elegance and beauty.

"Micah," I nearly whisper, filled with so many emotions. "It's stunning."

He kneels beside me, placing his hand on the small of my back. "It's not nearly as stunning as you."

Kissing him tenderly, I cup his face with my hand. "Can you help me put it on?"

"Of course."

He carefully removes the necklace from the box and secures it around my neck. Examining the sight of me wearing it, admiration flickers in his eyes.

"How does it look on me?" I ask, sheepishly smiling.

"Perfect," he murmurs.

"Alright, Damien," Jensen speaks up, leaning forward on the couch. "Let's see it."

His body visibly stiffens, and his jaw twitches.

Searching under the Christmas tree, I come across a black box with a red ribbon, delicately tied into a bow. Placing it onto my lap, I untie the bow, bouncing up and down like a little girl. The anticipation is literally killing me.

The moment I remove the lid, I fall silent. Still.

"Oh," I faintly say, hesitating. "It's empty."

"What," Jensen lets out, laughing.

Micah's eyes widen. "Yikes."

Damien's eyes meet mine, and there's something about his stare that leaves me unsettled. Uneasy. Although, I laugh it off, as well.

"You already gave me the best gift ever," I urge, rushing to my feet and plopping down on his lap. "Bringing me here, with all of you."

He looks away, wrapping his defined, tattooed arms around me. "I had something for you," he tells me, kissing my shoulder. "But it wasn't good enough."

"I'm sure that's not true," I object.

"I have something much better in mind," he states. "You'll just be getting it a little late."

"Like I said," I begin, briefly locking eyes with each one of them. Resting my head on his broad shoulder, I release a soft breath. "I already have all I need."

THE HEATED WATER of the hot tub hugs almost every inch of my skin, until Jensen bends me over, my stomach resting on the edge. My heart slams against my chest. His hips push into me, thrusting me forward. Heat shoots through my body, as his erection slips between my thighs, pressing against my clit. A hushed moan falls from my mouth while I grip the edge of the hot tub, keeping myself steady. Gripping my hips, he quickly thrusts forward, burying himself inside me.

Slamming his lubed cock into my tightness, over and over, he rocks my world. Sucking in a gasp, I push back against him, matching his thrusts. My tits bounce with every movement. My inner walls suck hard at his hard, thick cock. He grabs my shoulders, quickening his pace as he hammers into me.

Damien moves beside us and slips his hand between my thighs. My clit swells against his warm fingers, and I grind into his touch.

"Yes," I eagerly moan, edging Jensen on as he pumps into me harder.

"Your desperate little cries are my downfall," he grunts, caressing the branding of their initials on my hip with his thumb. "I'm going to come for you so fucking hard."

Tightly squeezing the edge of the hot tub, my eyes roll into the back of my head. And without warning, I explode, seeing stars behind my eyelids.

Jensen tenses up behind me as he finds his release, before lowering himself into the water, leaving me hunched over the edge.

Damien grabs my shoulder and turns me to him, as he leans his firm ass on the edge. Staring up at him through my eyelashes, I wait for his order. He holds himself at the base with his forefinger and thumb, the rest of his fingers curved around his balls.

"Suck," he commands, eyes narrowed.

Taking him into my mouth, my lips stretch wide. Cradling his thick cock with my tongue, my lips slide back and forth along his length. His body shudders, as he grabs the back of my head, plunging into the back of my throat.

Gagging on his dick, my stomach tightens.

"Yes," he says through clenched teeth.

A roar escapes from his chest as he pumps faster. Harder.

Gripping his hips, and bobbing my head, I meet each of his thrusts. Choking on his big cock, squeezing my eyes shut.

Air.

I need *air*.

My lungs burn from the lack of oxygen, and my head becomes light. Until, suddenly, he releases himself into the back of my throat in long spurts. Licking the tip of his crown, I savor the taste of him.

Blinking up at him, I submissively grin. "Did I do good, daddy?"

He takes hold of my jaw, grazing his thumb over my lips. "Yes," he confirms. "And now Micah is going to reward you."

Micah holds out his arms. "Come here, baby," he breathes, bringing me into his chest. "Sit on the ledge for me and lean your back against the window."

Doing as I'm told, I gasp from the feeling of the cold glass on my back. My nipples pucker into hard, red buds, and goosebumps rise on my skin.

"Spread your legs for me, sweetheart," he nearly whispers, and I obey.

He brings my ass to the very edge and buries his face between my thighs. Squirming against his warm mouth, he yanks me closer, deeply inhaling the scent of my arousal. He nibbles, licks, and sucks, completely devouring me. Lightly flicking my clit with his tongue, he groans into me. Squeezing his head between my thighs, my breathing quickens.

Pushing his finger inside of me, my pussy clenches around him, holding him captive. Raising my hips, I ride his face, and my clit begins to swell against his tongue. Adding in another finger, he thrusts deeper, curling them against my walls.

He moans, again and again, which pushes me to the brink of my orgasm. My back arches as he lightly sucks my clit. Fucking me with slippery fingers, he flattens his tongue, sending every nerve ending on edge.

"Mmm," he groans against my flesh, his shoulders tensing.

"Oh, yes, Micah," I cry out, convulsing. Whimpering.

Gasping for air, my climax entirely consumes me. He breathes hard and fast, sinking his fingers further inside of me, again and again.

"Fuck," he moans, removing his fingers, and dipping his tongue inside me.

"Micah," I gasp, watching him squirm as I run my fingers through his hair.

And with his face still buried between my thighs, he comes for me.

Hard.

NEW YEAR'S EVE

THE NEW YEAR awaits at midnight. Riding passenger in my friend's car, I take a moment to reflect on everything that has happened in my life over the last twelve months. My achievements in school. Good grades. Working through and overcoming my traumas. Stepping out of my comfort zone. My emotional progress. Developing healthier coping skills. Focusing on the friendships and relationships that matter most to me.

Meeting Damien, Jensen, and Micah.

"Fucking seriously?" Sarah mumbles, turning down the music and harshly tapping at the screen of her GPS. "This thing is such a piece of shit."

"I can use my phone instead," I offer, holding back laughter.

"Got it," she declares, making a sharp right turn as I grip the dashboard, bracing myself. "Can you hand me my cigarettes?"

Shuffling through her messy purse, I eventually come across them. "You really have to organize this thing," I babble, handing it to her.

Ripping the pack from my grasp, she rolls her eyes. "Oh, Quinn. Nothing in my life is ever organized. You know that." She sighs, placing a cigarette between her lips. "Lighter?"

Going through her bag once more, I dramatically hand her the lighter. "Anything else?"

"Yeah," she replies, angrily tapping at the GPS once more. "Find me a guy to hook up with tonight."

"I thought you were talking to Asa?"

She snorts, irritated. "Asshole," she states, rolling down the window before lighting her cigarette. "Just like usual. They all turn out to be assholes. Men suck."

Not mine.

Raising my eyebrows, I turn my head, gazing out the window. "That sucks. I'm sorry."

"It's whatever," she carelessly says, before growling in frustration. "Okay. Seriously? This thing sucks. I have no idea where I'm going."

Pulling out my phone and glancing down at the screen, I smile bright, quickly opening our group text.

Jensen

We're running a little late princess

Micah

What are you wearing?

Damien

Doesn't matter what she's wearing

We're just going to end up tearing it off

"QUINN," Sarah sings, shaking my shoulder. "We're lost."

Laughing quietly to myself over Damien's text, I type the address into the GPS on my phone. "Go straight through here," I direct. "Then take this next left."

"Is Damien coming?"

Swallowing hard, I nod. "Yeah."

"And let me guess. His friends are coming, too," she guesses.

"Yup."

"Why do they always tag along with him? It's kind of weird."

"Because I want them to."

She snorts under her breath, swerving around another car. "Why? They go everywhere with you guys. You'd think all four of you are together."

"We are," I confidently reply.

"You're fucking all three of them?" she gasps, bursting into laughter. "I'm so jealous. I don't even know what to say."

"Adam's street," I abruptly point out. "It's right up the hill."

"Don't change the subject," she rushes out, taking a long drag from her cigarette before flicking the ashes out the window. "You can't just tell me that you're in a four-way relationship and then not give me the details!"

"I sleep with them all. I go on dates with them all. I have feelings for all three of them. And yes, they're all incredible in bed."

"Which one makes you come, though? That's the real question," she says, laughing.

"They all do."

Her eyes widen as she shoots me a glare. "No way," she dully replies. "That's impressive. I can't even remember the last time a guy got me off."

"Seriously?"

"Sadly enough." She sighs, looking my way with a flirty smile. "Biggest dick?"

"They're all huge."

"Really?"

Smiling wide, I burst into laughter. "They're massive."

"I am so fucking jealous."

I laugh even harder.

"Have you ever been to a masquerade party?" she asks, shifting the subject.

"Nope."

"They had one last New Year's Eve. It was so crazy," she tells me. "I don't even remember how I got home."

"So, we keep these on the whole night?" I question, pulling down the visor to look in the mirror as I pull on my beautiful, silver mask that covers the top of my face.

"Yeah. Everyone is dressed in fancy clothes, too. Kyle's parents own this house but they're in Spain apparently, so he has it all to himself. He throws New Year's Eve parties every year. It's literally a mansion," she explains.

"Must be nice to have that kind of money."

"Right," she agrees. "Oh, you can turn off your GPS. I know where I am now. You're going to die when you see this place."

She was right.

Astonishment washes over me once we reach the front entrance, driving through the tall, opened gate. We're welcomed by trees decorated with bright, white lights as we make our way up the hill. Taking in every unique and gorgeous detail of the white mansion in the distance, a burst of adrenaline overwhelms me. There are cars parked in what seems like every direction. This place is packed.

"Great. No parking," Sarah dryly mumbles, before pulling into a spot on the grass. "This will do."

"This is insane."

"They have so many spare rooms in this house; usually people just crash here," she says, putting the car in park before checking her phone. "Wendy texted me. They're here."

Entering the house, a large, elegant entryway immediately welcomes us. There are tall ceilings, and two beautiful, spiral staircases, which are wrapped with garland and lights. There's also by far the biggest Christmas tree I've ever seen in my life. I'm left in awe as we make our way further inside, until something catches my wrist.

Spinning me around, I'm suddenly pulled against a firm chest.

"Excuse me," I rush out, stepping back, until his neck tattoos give him away. "Damien," I gasp, smiling.

He crookedly grins, bringing me closer. "You look stunning, Quinn," he seductively breathes.

My heart flutters while I study his black masquerade mask, sharp, tailored suit, and slicked-back hair. "Thank you," I sheepishly murmur, breathing in the intoxicating scent of his cologne. He always smells so good. I can't get enough.

My head spins, and my knees grow weak.

"Wow," Jensen says, stepping forward.

His gaze slowly travels down my breasts, sparkling black dress, and legs, before he locks his eyes with mine.

"You clean up really nice," I tell him, before turning to Micah, realizing they're all wearing the same black masquerade mask. "You all do."

"You're the most beautiful woman I've ever laid my eyes on," Micah says, pressing his lips against the back of my hand. "Now remind me. How did we manage to get so lucky?"

Damien grins.

Jensen smiles, his intense eyes fixated on mine.

And Micah simply stares, gawking at me in silence.

The way they make me feel is out of this world.

Sarah unexpectedly steps beside me, locking her arm with mine. "There you are," she says, enthusiastically. "I kept on walking and then realized you weren't still with me."

"No big deal."

"Damien," she purrs, looking him over.

He nods once, draping his arm around my waist. "Sarah."

"I need a drink," Jensen lets out, leading us down the hall.

It's nearly impossible to tell who anyone is, as the beautiful masks seem to hide everyone's identity. As we make our way further inside the party, everything becomes louder. There's chatter amongst guests, shouts of excitement from drinking games, laughter, and great music bursting through the speakers.

"I'm going to find the girls," Sarah tells me. "Or do you want to come with?"

Micah shakes his head. "We got her."

With that, she scurries away.

Damien and Jensen swiftly grab four champagne glasses off a platter from a server passing by. Accepting the glass from Damien, we raise a toast.

"To never looking back," Damien lets out. "And only looking forward."

Clink.

CHAPTER 8

The music blares through the surround sound speakers as everyone fills the dance floor. The energy is high, and the expensive champagne hits me at the perfect time. Kicking off my heels and pushing them off to the side, I grab Jensen's wrist, guiding him toward the large crowd of people. Dancing wildly, and singing loudly, we let loose and have the time of our lives.

White icicle Christmas lights are draped from the ceiling, with a mixture of black, silver, and gold balloons spread out around us. The sparkles of dresses and masks are illuminated by the lights, creating a beautiful glow in every direction.

Placing his hands on my hips, Jensen brings me against him, swaying me along to the rhythm. Eventually

Damien and Micah find us in the crowd, and we all dance together for what feels like hours.

Sweating and breathless, we make our way off the dance floor in laughter. Damien spots another waiter and grabs us more drinks, handing me a tall glass of champagne.

"This night couldn't get any better," I exclaim, tossing back the entire glass.

"Challenge accepted," Damien murmurs, staring at me with intense eyes.

I'm left captivated.

They lead me through the crowded first floor, up the spiraling staircase, and down a long, dimly lit hallway. It feels never-ending as my anticipation builds. My heart hammers. Micah pushes open a door, finding what appears to be a guest room. Once we enter through the doorway, he closes the door, locking it behind us.

"Get the fuck over here, Quinn," Damien orders, cocking his head to the side. "It's time to get fucked. Hard."

He aggressively grips the back of my head, tugging on my hair. For a moment, his eyes burn into me, and then he crushes his lips against mine. My fingers find their way to the hem of his dress pants, until he presses my back onto the bed.

My heart is pumping, and an ache settles between my legs. I'm desperate for their touch. To feel them deep inside of me. Before I can even make sense of it, my dress is yanked up to my waist, and Damien is stretching me wide, thrusting into me again and again. Biting out curses, sharply groaning, and pressing down on my throat, he takes my breath away.

It feels as if I'm floating, chasing after an earthshattering orgasm. It builds and builds within me. I've never been more desperate for release, and from the look in his eyes, I know that he sees it.

"Not yet, princess," Damien warns, pushing into me harder as he reaches between my thighs, pressing down on my pulsing clit.

"Please, Ghost," I choke out, my pussy spasming around him. "I'm so close—"

"Hold off, baby girl," he sharply exhales, increasing his pace, slamming his hips against mine. "I want to come with you."

"Please," I beg, squirming beneath his masculine body, digging my nails into his neck.

"Oh, fuck, baby," he groans, jolting my back into the mattress with each thrust. "Now, Quinn. Come with me, baby."

Crying out to him, and holding him close, we ride out our climax together. I'm a hot, quivering mess as he pulls himself out of me, and I'm unable to move, until Jensen pulls me onto him.

"Lean forward," he instructs, as I straddle his waist, arching my back.

A mixture of Damien and my cum seeps from my pussy. Micah catches it with his fingers, using it as lubricant as he sinks into my ass. My body slowly accepts him, inch by inch, although it feels as if I'm being split in half.

They both consume me, filling me completely. Fucking me savagely, they take what's theirs. My screams of pleasure echo off the wall of the room. Damien removes his tie, sliding it out from his collar before wrapping it around my wrist. He binds me to the headboard, both of my arms, grabbing my jaw and ensuring I look into his eyes.

"Look at me," he murmurs, slipping his thumb into my mouth. "I want to see that pretty look on your face when you come."

"Oh, God, yes," I breathlessly whimper, grinding myself against Jensen's pelvis.

"Your ass is so fucking tight," Micah grunts, thrusting into me faster, spreading my cheeks with his hands. "Such a pretty little hole."

"Ride Jensen's dick, baby," Damien commands, gathering my hair in his hand, holding it back. "Squeeze that perfect pussy around him, Quinn."

"Oh my God," I gasp, the fabric of their ties cutting into my wrists.

"My cock can't get enough of you," Jensen bites out, bucking his hips from the bed, hammering into me.

And suddenly, I'm right there, on the brink of the edge.

"Fucking take it," Damien urges, groaning under his breath as he watches me come. "Good girl," he praises, smacking my ass. "You're ours, Quinn." He sneaks his hand between my legs, rubbing my clit in slow, torturous circles as I climax again. "Don't you ever fucking forget that."

THE PARTY HAS COMPLETELY COME to life as we make our way back downstairs, only two hours left until the clock strikes midnight. Jensen hands me another tall glass of champagne, before raising his.

"What a great way to end the year," he says. "With a *bang*."

"I'll drink to that," I happily reply, taking a small sip until someone bumps into my shoulder, almost knocking me over.

"What the fuck, man," Micah snaps, and they're all on alert.

"Watch where the fuck you're going," Damien coldly threatens.

"My bad," the guy says. A royal blue mask hides his identity, and he apologetically holds up his hands. "I meant no harm. Wasn't watching where I was going—"

Suddenly, my glass falls from my grasp, shattering against the floor.

My heart hammers.

I'm no longer breathing.

I'm paralyzed with emotions I can't comprehend.

I feel like I'm going to be sick.

"Shit," the guy curses, moving closer as I step back, nearly dragging Micah in front of me in the process. "You okay?"

That *voice*.

I know that voice.

It's him.

Eric Spellman.

My rapist.

"Quinn?" Damien questions, his jaw clenched tight with concern.

"What's wrong?" Jensen asks, grabbing my arm.

And I flinch.

"Quinn," Damien repeats, louder.

"Quinn," Eric cheerfully lets out, as if nothing's happened between us.

As if he didn't ignore me when I begged him to stop. When I said no to him. Over and over. When I struggled beneath him the best that I could, while he pinned me against the stiff mattress. When he gave me no choice other than to take his invasion, whether I consented or not.

"It's good to see you again," he begins, until I turn fast on my heel.

Bolting toward the front door, I do the only thing I can think of in this moment.

This time, I escape.

CHAPTER 9

$\mathscr{M}$y whole world collapses around me as I run out into the night, embracing the cold, winter air. My chest tightens, and my vision becomes blurry. Bumping into several people on the front steps, I trip and fall onto the hard pavement, tearing the skin off my knees.

Gasping for air to fill my deprived lungs, tears fill my eyes. I can hear everyone asking if I'm okay while they try to help me to my feet, yet I swat them away, screaming out in hysteria.

"Quinn," Micah shouts from over my shoulder, quickly dropping to his knees beside me.

Stumbling back to my feet, I ignore his existence.

I can't breathe.

I can't think.

I can't wrap my head around any of this.

"You're bleeding," Jensen points out, gripping my arm to keep me steady.

"I want him dead," I begin to sob, hunching over as my knees finally give out, now throbbing with pain. "I want him fucking *dead*."

"Come here," Damien pleads, kneeling on the ground, pulling me into his arms.

"No," I refuse, and the pain from my trauma consumes me.

They were right. I never spoke a word about it to anyone, until I admitted it to them just a few days ago. I pretended it never happened. I never had the chance to move on. I never grieved.

Never healed.

And now, everything is coming back.

"Quinn," Micah quietly says, placing his hand on mine. "It's okay. You're okay, baby. We got you."

Blinking up at him through my tears of sorrow, I finally break down. Crying. Screaming. Slamming my shaking fists on his chest, he pulls me onto his lap, cradling me in his arms. Rocking me back and forth, soothing me. Protecting me.

"Is that him," Damien asks, barely any sound to his voice. "Is that him, Quinn?"

"Yes," I whisper. "It's him."

"Damien, wait," Jensen shouts, chasing after him.

"I'm so sorry," Micah softly says, holding the back of my head. "I'm so sorry, baby. You're okay. Everything's going to be okay."

"You promise?" I ask between sobs, while he carefully removes my mask.

"Yes, Quinn." He stares endlessly into my puffy, red eyes, and takes my face between his hands. "I promise."

Effortlessly lifting me into his arms, he carries me to the Jeep while I hold onto him for dear life. As he places me into the passenger seat, I push every thought and flashback into the back of my head, locking them away for good.

And within seconds, I become numb.

He fastens my seatbelt for me and dries my face with his sleeve. Just as he's about to shut my door, my fingers clasp around his wrist.

"Micah," I softly mutter, grasping the collar of his shirt and bringing him back to me. "Thank you," I whisper, wholeheartedly. "For always being here."

"I'm not going anywhere," he tells me, pressing a lingering kiss on my forehead.

"Micah."

His voice catches us off guard. Jensen grabs his shoulder, and even with the mask hiding his expression, the look in his eyes terrifies me. It's evident that something's wrong.

Micah shuts my door, facing his back to me. "Where's Damien?"

"I can't find him," he dryly replies, pulling him further away, until I can no longer hear them.

My ears begin ringing, and goosebumps rise on my skin. I've forgotten my jacket in Sarah's car. It's such a cold night; I'm able to see my own breath. My thoughts are in shambles. My knees are killing me. I'm still bleeding, and there's somehow dried blood on my hands. There's a full moon tonight. I wish I was curled up in bed.

Where is Ghost?

My mind races.

The sound of the driver's side door opening startles me, breaking me from my thoughts. Micah starts the engine, ensuring that the seat warmers and heat are on full blast.

"Is everything okay?" I softly ask. "What's going on?"

Jensen hops in the back.

Micah hesitates, and gently takes my hand. "Everything's fine," he reassures me.

"We're getting you out of here," Jensen says, reaching up to caress my cold arms, warming me with the friction.

"Where's Damien?"

"Don't worry about that," Micah dismissively answers, tightly gripping my thigh as he speeds down the long driveway. "He can handle himself. That, I'm sure of."

Somehow, over the drive, I've managed to lose track of time. Micah opens my door once we reach their apartment, and Jensen helps me onto my feet, ensuring I've gained back my balance.

"I'll be back," Jensen tells us, shutting my door before walking around to the driver's side.

"Where are you going?" I call out.

Micah wraps his arm around me, bringing me close.

"Back to the party, so I can bring the crazy bastard home," he rushes out, slamming his door.

"Come on," Micah calmly urges, guiding me toward the front steps.

THE BATHWATER IS the perfect temperature. Micah washes my back while I hug my scraped knees tight against my chest. Shutting my eyes, I drown in the feeling of the water soothing my skin and muscles. The warmth caresses me, filling my body with heat, even though I feel so cold.

Broken.

Empty.

It's such a strange feeling to know that I've unintentionally blocked out what had happened to me over a year ago now. Thinking back, I always thought I was crazy. I believed him when he told me that I wanted it. *Asked* for it.

And I never told anyone about it until I told Damien, Jensen, and Micah. They listened. They comforted me. They reassured me that it wasn't my fault.

Micah grazes the washcloth over my knees, and gently washes away the dried blood, staining the water pink. Staring at the concerned expression on his face, I find myself admiring him while he cleans my wounds. Every feature. Every detail.

The pained look behind his gentle eyes.

He cares about me so much.

They all do.

"Micah," I nearly whisper, and his eyes meet mine.

"Am I hurting you?" he questions.

Shaking my head, I lean forward and kiss him.

He lifts me from the bathtub, wraps a towel around my body, and dries me off, before carrying me to bed. Stepping out of his sweatpants and boxers, he climbs under the sheets beside me. Curling up closer, I press my naked body against his, taking in all the warmth he has to offer. Gently stroking my damp hair, he entangles our legs, bringing me closer.

His lips brush mine, so delicately my head starts to spin. An intense feeling builds up inside me, as he kisses me with passion. An undying longing. He runs his hands all over my body, exploring every inch of me.

Micah rolls onto me, pinning me beneath him, and kissing me with an urgency. Slowly stroking his cock, I bite his lip. He groans into my mouth, rocking his hips forward. Positioning himself at my entrance, he pushes in the tip, teasingly.

"Please," I breathe against his lips.

He sinks into me with one, long stroke, a quiet moan escaping us at the same time. Wrapping my legs around his waist, I accept him deeper, feeling him more fully. Slowly moving within me, he kisses me tenderly. Passionately. Pushing his fingers through mine, he presses the back of my hand to the pillow, holding me captive.

He trails his soft lips along my jaw, his chest pressed firmly against my breasts. We couldn't get any closer than this, yet, together, we've somehow become one. Sinking into me, again and again, his breathing quickens.

My head becomes light. My toes begin to curl, and my body trembles. My inner walls suck at his cock with each thrust, and before I know it, I'm already there.

Meeting my hips with his, my back arches, and my mouth falls open. My quiet cries fill the room as he rests his face in the crook of my neck.

"Quinn," he breathes against my skin, tightening his hold on me.

"Come with me, Micah," I beg.

And in perfect timing, we both come together.

CHAPTER 10

DAMIEN

*M*y phone continues to vibrate in my jacket pocket. Again, and again, despite how many times I've made it clear I don't intend to answer. In this moment, all I see is red. My blood boils in my veins, and all my senses are heightened.

So much fucking anger.

I need to find my release.

And I need it, now.

According to how closely I've been watching him, studying his every move, I know it's almost time for his smoke. Leaning against the doorway, I observe how uncomfortable the woman he's with is. Her body language screams it.

Yet, this prick just won't take no for an answer.

Clenching my jaw tight, my teeth are on the verge of shattering. My breathing hitches at the thought of him hurting Quinn. The moment images of the two of them begin to flood through my mind, I slam my hand against the doorway, startling several people beside me.

They scurry away, shooting me alarmed stares in the process.

He heads toward the front entryway, and I slowly creep behind him. Stalking my prey. Ready for revenge. Pushing open the door, he drunkenly stumbles out into the night.

Unfortunately for him, nobody else is anywhere in sight.

He lights up his cigarette, making his way toward the parked cars while I follow closely behind him. At first, I lurk in the shadows, until I intentionally step out beneath the light. Tripping over his own feet, he spins around, catching his fall by grabbing onto the hood of a car.

"Fuck," he slurs, and suddenly, he looks my way. "Oh, hey, man. Didn't see you there."

"No worries," I bite out, not taking my eyes off him.

"You want a smoke?" he asks, gesturing to the cigarettes in his jacket.

Shaking my head, I step forward, closing in on him. "I'm good," I smoothly press, the unexpected vibrating of my cell phone catching me off guard.

"You been here before?" he casually asks.

"First time."

"Bet," he mumbles, taking a swig of his beer.

The eerie silence between us confuses him. That is clear. I don't know how much longer I can hold off before ending his life. Although, as much as I'd like to kill him right here, I can't be reckless. I need to stick to the plan.

"You good, bro?" he cautiously asks, stepping back.

And I step forward. "Honestly?" I ask, high beams flashing on and off in the near distance. "Not even fucking close," I spit out, shoving him hard, his back slamming against a car with a loud thud. "But I will be." Winding back my arm, my fist collides with his nose, dropping him to the ground with one blow. Standing over him, I kick him in the face, ensuring he's knocked out cold. "When your blood is on my hands."

Jensen comes to a screeching halt beside us, jumping out of the Jeep like a mad man, stomping toward us. We quickly scan the area to ensure we haven't been seen.

"Grab his legs," he says, opening the back door. "Let's fucking do this."

ERIC SPELLMAN IS STILL unconscious while we drag him into the abandoned shed, the place we claimed as ours many years ago. There's no power here, out deep in the middle of the woods, so the floodlights are our only source of light. Everything is wrapped in plastic. The floors. Even the walls. Except for the wooden chair in the middle of the room.

Binding his limp body to the chair with ropes, anger erupts through me. I backhand him, again, and again, until his eyes flutter open.

A look of intense horror crosses his face as he looks over his surroundings.

"What the fuck," he slurs, suddenly panicking. "Where am I?" he demands, struggling to break free from the ropes. His horrified eyes meet mine. "What the fuck is this?"

"Shut the fuck up, you piece of shit," I threaten, pulling out my knife. "You really thought you could get away with it. With putting your filthy fucking hands on her—"

"Who?" he begs, eyes wide, like a deer caught in headlights.

"There's more than one, isn't there?" Jensen asks, hitting him hard.

Without warning, urine trickles down his ankle, pitter-pattering against the plastic covering on the floor.

I laugh, with no humor intended. "You're fucking pathetic," I spit out, jumping forward and pressing the tip of the blade against his throat.

"Please," he cries out, shaking, tears leaking from his eyes.

"Usually, I enjoy taking my time with my kills," I sharply breathe, ripping off his mask and glaring straight into his eyes. "But it's almost midnight, and we intend to make sure that you don't get one single fucking breath of the New Year."

Plunging my knife into his stomach, he lets out a low grumble. Twisting the blade inside his flesh, I cut into him further. Adrenaline consumes my entire being the moment I see the defeated look on his face.

Quinn unexpectedly comes to my mind, and I remember how hard she cried to us after telling us what he did to her.

Red. Red. Red.

That's all I fucking see.

Blood seeps through his white shirt, but it's not enough. Going into a fit of rage, I continue to stab him. Again, again, and again. Until I completely lose my mind, right on the verge of blacking out.

Dropping my knife to the ground, I push over his chair and straddle him. My fists slam against his face, over and over. Blood splatters everywhere, painting the walls. The sound of his bones crunching doesn't faze me. Doesn't make me stop. Even though at this point, he's unrecognizable.

"Damien," Jensen repeats, blow after blow. "Damien."

Yet, I can't seem to stop.

"He's dead," he loudly urges.

Holding up my fist, I lean back, staring down at the mess I've made in silence.

Contentment.

"What time is it?" I ask, savoring the sharp pains of my broken knuckles.

"We have time," he tells me.

"I almost blacked out again."

He looks down at the lifeless, unidentifiable body beneath me, and nods. "I know."

Quinn

My eyes flutter open.

"Damien," I breathe, wrapping my arms around him in a tight embrace.

He sits on the edge of the bed, holding me close. "I'm here," he whispers, tucking a strand of hair behind my ear. "I have your gift."

My eyes light up with excitement. "Really?" I ask.

Jensen enters the room, and Micah wakes up, leaning his back against the headboard.

"It's about time," Micah says, sarcasm thick in his tone.

Damien crookedly grins, retrieving the box from the nightstand, before placing it on my lap.

Carefully lifting the lid, my heart sinks at what's inside.

A royal, blue masquerade mask.

And suddenly, I *know*.

"We all have our demons," Damien says, grazing his fingertips over the initials carved into my skin on my hip. "And sometimes, they consume us."

"You did this," I begin, setting the box back onto the nightstand. "For me?"

His eyes burn into mine. "I'd do anything for you."

With one swift motion he grabs the back of my neck, crushing his lips on mine. He kisses me hard, feverishly. Bringing me against his firm body as I dissolve into him. My stomach flutters, and the most beautiful emotions consume me. My arms find their way around his neck, and I hold him so tight.

Jensen and Micah move behind me, stroking my backside with their warm hands, kissing their way down my neck and shoulders. There's a spark between the four of us, an electrical current in the air. Something's changed.

Which was once lust, now turns into an undying passion.

Damien groans into our heated kiss, grazing his lips down my jaw. "Quinn," he emotionally whispers, staring down at me with vulnerable eyes.

"I know," I whisper back, trembling.

"Are you cold?"

"No," I rush out, bringing him closer. "I'm melting."

"That's it, baby," Micah purrs, pressing a tender kiss on my shoulder.

"Our good girl," Jensen says beside my ear, and I shut my eyes, drowning in pure bliss.

"Melt for us," Damien breathes.

ACKNOWLEDGMENTS

Chris,

Your love and support means the world to me, as always.

Kayla,

I couldn't have asked for a better friend. Truly. Thank you for everything, times a million.

Amanda,

Thank you for hyping me up when I impulsively quit my job to focus on writing full-time. You made me realize it's never too late to dream big.

Charity Chimni,

You spoil me so much and I'm okay with thaT. What would I ever do without you?

To my beta readers,

Thank you for dedicating your time to me! For giving me such helpful feedback! And for loving Quinn and these masked men, just as much as I do, if not more!

To my ARC team,

You all rock! The outpouring of reviews I've received has left me in awe. I'm so happy you all love these characters and their story. Thank you for helping me promote, for building up the hype, and for putting such a huge smile on my face every step of the way.

To my readers,

My dream has always been to become a full-time author, and because of you, it's finally come true! Thank you, from the bottom of my heart!

ABOUT THE AUTHOR

Molly Doyle's passion for writing began in her fifth grade English class. After turning to an online writing platform in 2013, Molly's works have gained the attention of more than 43 million readers. When she's not binge watching Supernatural, acting in Haunt Attractions, or drinking wine near the fireplace, she's writing Erotic Romance novels and dreaming of one day becoming a Director and Screenwriter.

More than 27 million reads online.
First time in print.

Molly loves to hear from her readers! You can reach her on social media or at realmollydoyle@yahoo.com or www.realmollydoyle.com.

f facebook.com/authormollydoyle
instagram.com/realmollydoyle
tiktok.com/@authormollydoyle

Printed in Great Britain
by Amazon